Dawn of Surrender

Also by Liliana Hart

THE MACKENZIE SERIES
Dane
A Christmas Wish: Dane
Thomas
To Catch A Cupid: Thomas
Riley
Fireworks: Riley
Cooper
A MacKenzie Christmas
MacKenzie Box Set
Cade
Shadows and Silk
Secrets and Satin
Sins and Scarlet Lace
The MacKenzie Security Series *(Includes the 3 books listed above)*
1001 Dark Nights: Captured in Surrender
Sizzle
Crave
Troublemaker
Scorch
Spies and Stilettos
Sweet Surrender
Dawn of Surrender
The Promise of Surrender

THE GRAVEDIGGERS SERIES
The Darkest Corner
Gone To Dust
Say No More

Dawn of Surrender

A MacKenzie Family Novella

By Liliana Hart

1001 Dark Nights

EVIL EYE
CONCEPTS

Dawn of Surrender
A MacKenzie Family Novella
By Liliana Hart

1001 Dark Nights

Copyright 2017 Liliana Hart
ISBN: 978-1-945920-55-4

Foreword: Copyright 2014 M. J. Rose

Published by Evil Eye Concepts, Incorporated

Dedication

To all the readers who love the MacKenzies. I hope you keep a little piece of Surrender in your hearts forever.

Acknowledgments from the Author

A huge thanks to the team at 1001 Dark Nights! I couldn't ask for more amazing people to work with, and what makes it better is that they're friends. So to Liz, MJ, Jillian, Kim, and everyone who makes this such an incredible experience, thank you from the bottom of my heart. It's been a pleasure and an honor.

A huge thanks to my husband, Scott, who goes above and beyond in all things husband. He listens to me work my way out of corners I've written myself into, smiling and nodding. He keeps me hydrated with endless Route 44 Sonic drinks, and he doesn't sleep until I do when I'm on deadline. He's the best support system a girl could ask for. I'm lucky to have married a real life hero.

I also want to thank my children. They really are the most incredible people, who have learned to adjust accordingly to the odd eccentricities, writing and deadline schedules kept by their mother. I'm grateful they love pizza and hot dogs, but I'm also grateful for the privilege of raising some of the finest people I know.

Sign up for the 1001 Dark Nights Newsletter
and be entered to win a Tiffany Key necklace.

There's a contest every month!

Go to www.1001DarkNights.com to subscribe.

As a bonus, all subscribers will receive a free
1001 Dark Nights story
The First Night
by Lexi Blake & M.J. Rose

One Thousand and One Dark Nights

Once upon a time, in the future…

*I was a student fascinated with stories and learning.
I studied philosophy, poetry, history, the occult, and
the art and science of love and magic. I had a vast
library at my father's home and collected thousands
of volumes of fantastic tales.*

*I learned all about ancient races and bygone
times. About myths and legends and dreams of all
people through the millennium. And the more I read
the stronger my imagination grew until I discovered
that I was able to travel into the stories… to actually
become part of them.*

*I wish I could say that I listened to my teacher
and respected my gift, as I ought to have. If I had, I
would not be telling you this tale now.
But I was foolhardy and confused, showing off
with bravery.*

*One afternoon, curious about the myth of the
Arabian Nights, I traveled back to ancient Persia to
see for myself if it was true that every day Shahryar
(Persian: شـــهریار, "king") married a new virgin, and then
sent yesterday's wife to be beheaded. It was written
and I had read, that by the time he met Scheherazade,
the vizier's daughter, he'd killed one thousand
women.*

Something went wrong with my efforts. I arrived in the midst of the story and somehow exchanged places with Scheherazade — a phenomena that had never occurred before and that still to this day, I cannot explain.

Now I am trapped in that ancient past. I have taken on Scheherazade's life and the only way I can protect myself and stay alive is to do what she did to protect herself and stay alive.

Every night the King calls for me and listens as I spin tales. And when the evening ends and dawn breaks, I stop at a point that leaves him breathless and yearning for more. And so the King spares my life for one more day, so that he might hear the rest of my dark tale.

As soon as I finish a story... I begin a new one... like the one that you, dear reader, have before you now.

Chapter One

Montana, 1892

For all intents and purposes, Elizabeth MacKenzie should've died on a Tuesday.

The bank was stifling despite the beginnings of a blizzard outside. As it was almost closing time, they'd already shut the windows and the brazier was burning hot in the corner. Sweat was dripping in some very unladylike places. Not that anyone in Surrender would call her a lady, but it had never mattered much what other people thought.

There was a line of customers who'd waited until the last minute to do their business for the day. Most were shop owners who knew this would be their last chance to make a deposit before the storm shut everything down. And everything would be shut down. With luck, it would only be for a couple of days. At worst, it could be a couple of weeks.

She worried about the cattle and the ranch, but she knew her foreman and the ranch hands would take good care of everything. Even if she wanted to make it back home, there was no way to do it safely. The storm had already found

Surrender.

She watched the gray clouds roll toward them through the western wall of windows, the mountains no longer visible and the snow swirling in several directions. The wheeze of the wind could be heard through cracks in the windows and door. The atmosphere in the room was fraught with tension. No one spoke, and everyone was wondering how long they had to see to necessities before things got so bad they had to find shelter in town.

There were only two tellers behind the counter, Leroy Henry and Miss Adelaide Murchison. Lizzie had seen the bank manager, Samuel Peabody, peek out from his office once and then close the door. Lord knew, if work was involved Samuel was the first to disappear.

Leroy barely came up to Elizabeth's shoulders, and his body was so round he often gave the impression that he rolled from place to place instead of using his feet to walk. Miss Adelaide was unusually tall for a woman, almost a head taller than Elizabeth, and she had a long, hawk-like nose that made it seem as if she were looking down at everyone she talked to.

Leroy was a sweet man, but he worked at half the pace of Miss Adelaide. No one had ever called Miss Adelaide sweet. She was the meanest, most contrary woman Elizabeth had ever known. She'd take slow Leroy over Miss Adelaide any day of the week.

Elizabeth tapped the toe of her boot impatiently and tried not to fidget. She'd never been very good at waiting, especially when her plans involved a romantic night with her husband in the Surrender Hotel. Between the ranch and his duties as sheriff and dealing with her father's death, they hadn't taken time for a honeymoon.

In many ways, Cole was still a stranger to her. And she knew she was like a stranger to him too. She was more than capable of admitting that she wasn't like any other woman. And maybe that's why their marriage had gotten off to an unusual start. But she had to think her uniqueness was part of the reason Cole married her.

It had been Cole's suggestion to take two nights away from everything. And the timing with the storm had worked out beautifully. No one was going much of anywhere over the next two days, and they could spend the time devoted to each other instead of the needs of everyone else.

She and Cole had been two very independent people when they'd married. Elizabeth had never planned to marry at all, but her father's foresight had protected her and the ranch that had belonged to her grandfather. Of course, she hadn't realized that her father had asked Cole to marry her if he passed away. And she'd *thought* her father hadn't known she'd been in love with Cole MacKenzie since she was a young girl. But he'd known.

In his own way, he'd played matchmaker to make sure she'd gotten everything she wanted and still had control of the ranch. If her father hadn't deeded the ranch to Cole after he'd agreed to marry her, then it would've been taken from her. The bank would've put it up for sale to the highest bidder and she would've been left with nothing. Women couldn't own land in this part of the country. But their husbands could. And what she'd needed was a husband to keep her life from changing.

And though she'd been in love with Cole for years, he was a good dozen years older than she was. She couldn't help but wonder… If her father had never approached Cole about marrying her, would he have noticed her at all?

She was hoping more than anything that the two days they spent together would give them a marriage like her parents. Cole had been a good husband. He was kind and patient, but he was distant. They circled each other, never knowing what to say, so they didn't say anything and went on about their lives.

The only time she really felt like they were speaking the same language was when they made love. They had no miscommunications there. What she needed was to know that Cole loved her, and that she was more than just a favor he was fulfilling for her father.

But her time with Cole couldn't start until she'd finished her errand at the bank.

"Next." Miss Adelaide's shrill voice echoed in the building.

Drat. Elizabeth could've sworn she heard the person behind her sigh in relief that they weren't getting stuck with Miss Adelaide. On the plus side, Elizabeth would get out much faster and she could be on her way to the hotel. She straightened her spine and moved toward the old bat's window.

"Good afternoon, Miss Adelaide," Elizabeth said sweetly.

"Elizabeth," Adelaide said sourly. "What's your business?"

"I need to make a withdrawal."

"Does your husband know about this?" Her pale blue eyes narrowed menacingly.

"Yes, he does. But I'm not withdrawing from our personal account. I'm withdrawing from the ranch account."

"Hmmph," she said. "I think your father must have been losing his mind in his last days. And for your poor husband to go along with it…" Adelaide shook her head with disdain, but took the paper Elizabeth slid toward her so she could start the withdrawal process. "What kind of man lets his wife have that kind of control over the finances? Certainly not one I want acting as sheriff come election time. If a man can't control his wife, he surely can't control the population."

"So you've said before," Elizabeth said, her face flushing hotly because Adelaide was talking loud enough for everyone left in the bank to hear.

"This is a sizeable amount of money." Adelaide pursed her lips tightly as she studied the withdrawal form. "More than you usually take out. I don't know what you're planning, but you can be sure that I'll keep him informed. I won't allow any funny business on my watch. And you're just the type of woman to take something right out from under your husband's nose and do what you want with it. Your father gave you too much freedom growing up, letting you wear men's clothes and learning to shoot and rope cattle. You've got too much independence and not enough sense. You'd think you were a man with the way you conduct yourself. Your mama must be rolling over in her grave to see what you've become."

"I'm sure Mama is resting peacefully," Elizabeth said between gritted teeth. "Now if you don't mind, I've got an appointment I need to keep."

If she didn't get out of this bank soon, her own husband was going to have to arrest her for murder.

"You didn't tell me what you needed the withdrawal for," Adelaide said stiffly.

"Oh, I thought you knew already. Everyone else in town has been talking about it." Elizabeth looked at her with pity and then instantly felt remorse. She just couldn't sink to Adelaide's level. "We're ready to build the new barn. All the supplies are in at the lumber mill."

"I guess Sheriff MacKenzie lets you run as wild and free as your father did. It's no wonder he's been looking for outside work to distance himself from you. Your ways will ruin a man like Cole MacKenzie."

Adelaide's smile was full of spite, and Elizabeth knew she was luring her into a trap. But it was an arrow that hit a little too close to the bullseye. And Adelaide knew it.

"But Cole is a smart man," Adelaide continued. "I heard a US Marshal was in town and they've been talking all day. It's only a matter of time before he pins that star to his vest and takes off to parts unknown. His skills are so renowned that the president sent his top man to recruit him. You wouldn't want to hold him back, would you? It's not like you've got a bump growing under those trousers you insist on wearing. Doesn't seem to me like Cole MacKenzie has much of a reason to stay in Surrender at all."

Elizabeth knew she was pale. And her hand shook slightly as she reached out to take the money. Once she'd secured it in her bag, she took a step back and decided the best course of action was to just walk away. But she couldn't do it this time. No one ever stood up to Adelaide. The people of Surrender just let her spew vitriol and then walked away with their tails tucked between their legs.

Talking back would only lead to more trouble. The rumors would be vicious. And it wasn't only herself she had to think about. Cole was an important man in town, and he had a great deal of responsibility. She didn't want to hurt his reputation more than she probably had already. But she just couldn't stand by any longer.

"Adelaide Murchison," Elizabeth said with a slight quiver to her voice, but it was loud enough to catch everyone's attention. "You are the most hateful, spiteful woman I've ever had the misfortune to meet. I remember your parents from when I was a child, and they were some of the nicest people I've ever met. So if you want to talk about people rolling in their graves then maybe you should look a little closer to home."

Someone gasped from behind her, and Leroy Henry's eyes were big and round behind his spectacles.

"You don't know me or my husband, and you never knew the kind of man my father was, because he couldn't stand to be in a room with you and share the same air. But know this," she said, her voice ringing in the deafening silence. "You'll reap your reward. You're so busy judging and gossiping about everyone else that you've forgotten the sermon Reverend Graham has preached on several times. You might think that you're ruling your little part of earth, but your judgment day is coming. And you should be afraid because you're about the most un-Christian woman I've ever laid eyes on."

Adelaide gasped and clutched a hand to her breast, and Elizabeth nodded righteously. She felt vindicated and remorseful at the same time. She'd never backed away from a fight in her life, but it wasn't in her nature to be cruel. And she was sure she'd have to do penance for it later. But later seemed like a long ways off.

"I pray that you find peace somewhere in your soul and that your bitterness no longer eats you alive." With that, Elizabeth nodded her head once to Adelaide, did the same to Leroy, and turned on her heel to walk out of the bank, avoiding the wide-eyed stares of everyone else.

She pulled on the door, and it blew open with a hard gust of wind and snow. A man dressed in a nice suit and long wool overcoat, a hat pulled low over his eyes, was trying to get inside just as she was leaving, and they shuffled awkwardly around each other. He muttered a "Beg your pardon," and then moved to the side so she could get by.

The door closed behind her and her only thought was finding her husband. If Miss Adelaide was right, he had some explaining to do.

Chapter Two

Cole MacKenzie knew there was going to be trouble the minute the man walked through the door of the sheriff's office.

He wasn't a big man—maybe five foot nine in his boots—and his frame was on the thin side. *Average* was the word that came to mind. Followed closely by *deadly*. His duster was coated with a layer of grime and snow from a hard ride, and Cole saw the two pistols, one on each hip, as he walked toward him. He also saw the US Marshal's star pinned to his vest.

He pulled down the bandana that had protected his face from the storm and said, "Sheriff MacKenzie?" He pushed his hat back slightly so Cole could see his eyes. The eyes never lied.

Cole sighed, confident in his original observation that the man was going to be trouble. He didn't bother to remove his feet from his desk or stand up to greet the man properly. Others had come for him, and they'd all left without completing their mission.

"I'm Cole MacKenzie," he said. "And I'm not interested."

The man grinned, but Cole saw it in the wrinkling of his eyes since his mustache was so bushy it covered his lips. The marshal removed his hat and hung it on the rack next to Cole's, and then he did the same with his duster, clearly planning to make himself at home.

"You never know what you might be interested in until you know what you're interested in," the man said cryptically.

"Deep thoughts," Cole said.

With the hat and coat gone, Cole took a closer inventory of the man. He was younger than he'd first assumed, his hair a rich black in need of a trim. The drooping mustache was peppered with gray, making him seem older than he was. His eyes were a soft green, but Cole recognized the look in them—they were eyes that had seen too much—eyes that were a window to a broken soul.

Cole's eyes were blue, but he saw that same look in the mirror every morning, though since he'd married Elizabeth, the broken pieces had started to stitch themselves together again. But still, like recognized like.

The man was dressed much like Cole—black trousers, black vest, and a white shirt—though Cole had his sleeves rolled up. He hated anything constricting his movements if he needed to reach for his gun.

"You got any coffee?" the man asked. "I've missed out on a few nights of sleep to get here. I didn't think I'd make it once the snow started. I have to admit, I'm looking forward to a hot meal and a bed."

"You can get everything you want over at the Surrender Hotel," Cole said, seeing the weariness in the man's eyes. "I was just about to head over there myself to meet my wife. Things in town have already started to shut down. I'll drink a cup of coffee with you while you get a hot meal."

"I'd be grateful for the company since you're the reason I'm hungry and tired to begin with."

There was still a glimmer of laughter in the man's eyes, and Cole decided they'd get along just fine if the marshal was there for any other reason. It wasn't like Cole had gotten a lot accomplished throughout the day. His thoughts had been on his wife since he'd kissed her good-bye that morning, and he'd been restless and looking at the clock ever since. He couldn't decide if it was because a blizzard was coming to town or because he was afraid of what might happen when he and Elizabeth were stuck in a room together for two days.

He didn't know much about marriage. He and his brother hadn't had a very good example to go by. But he knew he loved his wife, and there was nothing more important than seeing a smile on her face. And he'd failed somewhere along the way. More often than not he'd catch her staring at him—a sadness or longing in her eyes—and he knew he was losing her. What he didn't know was how to fix it.

The last year had been difficult for Elizabeth. Her father, John Ross, had known he was sick, and he'd spoken to Cole about his wishes for them to marry and for the ranch to be passed to Cole since Elizabeth couldn't directly inherit. The thing was, Cole would've eventually asked Elizabeth to marry him—once he found time in his schedule. Sometimes the job took him away for days at a time if there was a manhunt or if someone needed to be tracked.

He'd wanted to give Elizabeth a little more time to grow into herself. She was barely twenty years old, but she knew how to run the ranch from the ground up. And Cole had promised John that he'd let Elizabeth run the ranch as she saw fit. The hiring, firing, herding, and selling of cattle were all her decisions. Not to say that he didn't lend a strong back from time to time. It was a legacy that would be passed down to their children and grandchildren after all.

But he felt like Elizabeth was carrying the weight of the world on her shoulders. She'd never really grieved her father's passing. Then they'd gotten married before there was even time for a funeral. And though they'd known each other and were friendly, they hadn't known each other like people who were to be married should. It had been a chaotic time, and they'd immediately gone from wedding, to funeral, to trying to make their lives seem normal. Elizabeth had thrown herself into getting the ranch in order, watching men she'd known since she was a child pack their bags and leave because they wouldn't take orders from a woman.

He'd stood by helpless, not knowing how to draw her in, how to make things better, and instead, he'd just focused on what he knew. And that was law and order. By any means necessary. And though they'd made a physical connection that was unlike anything he'd ever experienced, it wasn't enough for him.

It was Elizabeth's longtime foreman, Lester, who'd taken pity on Cole and pulled him aside when he'd asked what he should do. Lester had told him it was time to take charge and not be too passive in Elizabeth's grief. She was a strong woman—independent—and she'd move ahead on her own if Cole didn't act as if he wanted to move forward together.

They'd never had a honeymoon, and Lester said it was long past time they did. Cole didn't even think Elizabeth realized that the next day would mark a year of their marriage. And though they couldn't take a lot of time away and leave

Surrender, they could hole up with a soft bed, a tub that ran its own hot water, and food delivered to their doorstep. And maybe by the time they left the Surrender Hotel, they'd know exactly who the real Cole and Elizabeth MacKenzie were.

"You still with me?" the man asked.

"Just took a side trip," Cole answered. "It's been a long day."

"If you ask me, you've got the look of a man who has a woman on the brain."

"I knew you'd be trouble the minute you walked in the door."

"And I've got a real winning personality too."

Cole couldn't help but laugh. He stood and glanced through the big plate glass windows that gave him a perfect view of his town. He'd already sent out men to tell everyone to close things down early. There was already a foot of snow on the ground, but visibility had gotten worse as the day progressed.

"You got a name?" Cole asked the man. "I like to know who I'm saying no to."

The man's droopy mustache lifted again. "My apologies. After finding you, coffee and a bed were the only things on my mind. And maybe a woman, but I think I'm too tired for that."

"Probably a good thing," Cole said. "Those kind of women more than likely have a line of customers. It is a blizzard after all."

"Good point. Besides, I'm not like the others. I'm a lot harder to say no to. The name's Jesse Calhoun."

Cole felt a shiver of something he couldn't explain run up his spine—excitement?—anticipation? Jesse Calhoun was probably the most notorious lawman in the country. He was a legend.

Cole put his hat and duster on while Jesse did the same, then he grabbed the overnight bag he and Elizabeth had packed that morning. He opened the door and held it steady so it wasn't blown into the wall. The cold slashed at his exposed skin like a knife. He closed the door behind them, but he didn't bother to lock up. Carl would be there before long and would bunk in the back room. If there were any emergencies, he would see to things.

He ducked his head against the wind as they made their way across the street. He hadn't uttered a word since Jesse had told him his name. Questions raced through his mind. Why was President Harrison so desperate to recruit him as a US Marshal that he'd send the man with the highest kill and capture rate to hunt him down? Maybe it was symbolic. But everyone knew who Jesse Calhoun was, and the gut feeling that had saved his life more than once in battle was stirring uncomfortably.

"Nothing but trouble," he muttered under his breath.

"What's that?" Jesse asked, still grinning. "I don't think I heard you right. Wind's too loud."

"This is a bad one. Hope you're planning to stay a few days. If you hadn't come in when you did, we'd be discovering your body in a snow drift in a few weeks. A hell of a way to go."

Jesse shivered and shook his head. "I don't know how you stand it. This Texas boy wouldn't last long up here. I'm out of my territory. It's March. Snow for that many months in a row would make me crazy."

"It makes a lot of people crazy. The start of spring is always my busiest time of year. People are tired of being cooped up, and they're tired of the cold. And you can only do so much of the one thing that keeps two people both warm and out of trouble, though that sometimes leads to plenty of trouble in itself."

Jesse laughed. "People can always find plenty of trouble. Too hot, too cold, or just the wrong day of the week. Sometimes makes you wonder why we even bother at all."

"Someone's got to," Cole said, but he felt the weariness of the responsibility they'd been taxed with. Especially in this part of the country. People wanted to take care of their own in their own way, no matter the result. And then there were others who wanted to take advantage of the remote area and difficult terrain.

"You've got yourself a nice town here," Jesse said. "Lots of progress coming through."

Surrender was more than a nice town. It had become his home like no place ever had before. His soul had connected with Surrender the moment he'd seen it—a hidden jewel of hills and valleys and crystalline lakes, when it wasn't covered in a layer of white. He didn't know how long he'd sat at the top of the hill just looking down at it, the sun at his back and his future in front of him.

It had grown since he'd become sheriff, mostly because of the railroad they'd built just outside of town. The last train had left early that morning, and there wouldn't be another until the storm had passed.

The main street was lined on each side with wooden buildings that had all been white-washed to match. The Surrender Hotel sat right in the middle across the street from the sheriff's office, and it was three full stories, with fancy glass that had been brought in all the way from Boston. The lights inside were a beacon through the increasingly heavy snow.

The street was newly cobbled, but it didn't make much difference with the snow. There were hitching posts and watering troughs, but there was no sign of life on the street other than the two of them.

Along with the hotel and the sheriff's office, the other businesses located along each side of the cobbled street were a blacksmith shop, mercantile, haberdashery, gunsmith, apothecary, and a saloon. There was even a lawyer from back east who'd put up his shingle after the railroad was finished. And he was glad to see everything was dark inside each of the businesses and everyone had gone home.

There was a livery stable with a large paddock set some ways back because the area was often congested with wagons and horses. The bank was located on the other side of the livery, but far enough away to avoid the smell. And at the very end of the street was a white-steepled church, with a bell that was rung on the hour while the train was running. He hated that bell.

Surrender was the closest place to shop, restock, or trade for a lot of folks in the area. Otherwise, it was a three-day ride to Billings.

"We're going to have to make some changes soon," Cole acknowledged. "With progress comes problems. It's too much progress for a lot of the folks here. The railroad changed everything. Too many transients. Too much money with the business people coming in from the cities. That means more crime. Train robberies have been as much of a concern as stagecoach robberies."

"You're going to need more people," Jesse said.

"I know. I've got two deputies, but I've put out the word for more. Will probably have to bring them in from the city. Men out here are already working their own farms and ranches. They're not going to give that up for the little we can offer them."

The Surrender Hotel had a wide front, the windows on the left displaying a parlor where guests could gather after dinner, and the windows on the right displaying the restaurant. The double doors were painted bright blue and there were wooden barrels where there were usually flowers planted, but the barrels were filled with snow.

They went inside and were enveloped in immediate warmth. The staircase was a showcase of polished wood that went up three floors. The carpet was the same shade of blue as the front door, and all the wall paneling was white. There was a crystal chandelier that the owner, Gerald Clark, had brought back with him all the way from Paris, France. The art and other decorations were much fancier than Cole ever preferred, but those who visited the hotel always seemed impressed. There was a long counter to the right of the stairs and keys and mail slots were on the wall behind it.

"Sheriff," Will Clark greeted them as they entered. "We've been expecting you. Are you dining with us tonight?"

"Yes, but I'm going to wait for my wife," Cole said. "I'll join the marshal here for coffee while he eats."

Will was a young man, in his late teens, with dark red hair, bright blue eyes, and a ruddy complexion. His parents owned the hotel. They also owned the mercantile and ran the bank. And Will looked at Jesse Calhoun with a mix of awe and hero worship.

Will was fascinated with tales of the Earp brothers and

Wild Bill Hickok. Any time a marshal came through town, Will would hunt him down and ask question after question about what being a lawman was really like. Cole had the feeling that Will would be off on his own adventure if his parents didn't have such a tight rein on him.

"Sure thing, Sheriff," Will said excitedly. "I've got your room all ready for you just like you asked. It's the best we have to offer. Even has a big porcelain tub from back east with hot running water." Then he turned his attention to Jesse. "And I've got just the room for you, too, Marshal. I'd put you next to the sheriff since y'all are friends, but my pa told me not to put anyone in the rooms around the sheriff's so he and his wife have privacy. But you'll have a real good view of the whole street from the second floor. That way you can keep an eye on everybody."

"I appreciate that," Jesse said dryly. And then he looked at Cole with raised brows, and Cole felt the heat rising in his cheeks.

"We'll take the seat by the front window," he told Will, desperate to change the subject. "And keep the coffee coming. It's been a long, cold day."

"And I'll have whatever the special is," Jesse said. "I'm so hungry I could eat just about anything."

Will nodded as if he had access to Jesse's deepest, darkest secrets. "I bet you haven't had time to eat or sleep trying to catch The Silver Creek Bandits. I heard about what happened in Denver. I figure they headed into the mountains to lay low until they're ready to hit the next bank."

Will stopped talking and all the color drained from his face. "Oh, no. You think they're going to hit Surrender next, don't you? That's why you're here. I told my father that we'd be a target ever since they put in the new railroad. We've got too much gold for our own good."

"Take a breath, Will," Cole said easily, slapping the boy on the shoulder. "Jesse's just in for a visit to see me. We've got a lot of catching up to do."

"Oh," Will said, only slightly deflated. "I'm sure you know a lot of important people with you being a war hero and all, but Surrender has never had so many marshals come through town before. I think something is going on, and you're just keeping it a secret."

"Lots of sugar for the coffee," Cole said, cutting Will off. "Marshal Calhoun is about to fall asleep standing up."

"Right, right." Will jerked to attention. "Sorry about that. Take a seat and I'll have you served up in no time." With that, he scurried toward the kitchen door.

Cole and Jesse wiped their boots and hung their hats and coats on the rack, and then headed toward the table in front of the big plate glass window. They both positioned their chairs so they could see outside and anyone who might come into the restaurant.

"You don't want anyone next to your room, huh?" Jesse asked, laughter in his eyes.

"Shut up, Calhoun."

"I've never seen a lawman blush like that. Must be a special occasion."

"We're just taking some time away, that's all," Cole insisted. "Everyone in town will be standing outside our door by the time Will spreads the word. Nobody can keep a secret in this damned town, and everyone is nosy as hell."

"Good thing you're about to get snowed in," Jesse said, waggling his eyebrows.

"I wish I didn't like you so much. I'd punch you right in that smug smile."

"I told you I had a winning personality," he said. "For some reason, no one ever believes me. You know, Will's not far off about The Silver Creek Bandits. You heard what they did in Denver?"

"I heard," Cole said, his blood running cold. "Twelve dead. They strike right at the end of the day. They never leave any alive. And they're gone before anyone can stop them, and no one seems to know the details. They're like ghosts."

"You're partially right," Jesse agreed. "But it wasn't twelve. Body count was twenty this time."

Cole whistled. "That's the biggest one yet. They're escalating. That puts the death toll at more than fifty."

"The stakes are higher. They don't want to stop robbing the banks, but it's getting harder to conceal themselves so they're going to greater lengths for the cover-up. There was a witness that saw them go into the bank in Denver. He was able to give a good description of three of the men. The sheriff in Denver tried to keep the witness under wraps, but word always gets out. You know how fast gossip can spread. Everyone knew there was a witness before the last sketch was drawn, so you can bet The Silver Creek Bandits knew too."

"What happened to the witness?" Cole asked, already knowing the answer.

"His name was Jedidiah Taylor. Had his throat slit in his own bed. Along with his wife and two boys. We'll never have another witness come forward. In fact, I think the only reason Jed came forward was because the local sheriff promised him protection."

"He failed."

Jesse nodded. "But not for lack of trying. There were four deputies stationed outside of the Taylors' home. They didn't fare any better than Jedidiah and his family."

They paused their conversation as a server came in with the coffee tray and a small loaf of crusty bread and fresh butter. Jesse drank his coffee black, with no sugar, and Cole watched a little life come back into his eyes. He attacked the bread with the vigor of a man who hadn't seen anything but jerky or canned beans for the better part of a couple of weeks.

"Why'd you really come?" Cole asked. "Other marshals have come before you. They've all given me the same spiel about how my country needs me and what an honor it is to serve the president. What's changed? You're the best there is. Why'd he send you?"

"I'm the best marshal there is," Jesse said matter-of-factly. "And there are others who are almost as good as I am. But we've got a bigger problem on our hands than just one or a few men can handle. You're faster with a gun than I am and you're a better tracker. President Harrison asked who the best person was to hunt down The Silver Creek Bandits and I told him you. So he sent me to convince you."

Cole felt the tug of duty and responsibility, but he coldly pushed it away. He'd done his time for his country. Now he owed it to his wife and community to put in the time for them. He'd be lying if he said it wasn't an honor to be wanted for the job, or that the notoriety wouldn't feed his ego. But he wasn't a hot-headed young man anymore with a quick trigger finger. He'd learned there were things more important in life than notoriety.

Jesse sighed and put down the bread he'd been in the process of buttering. Then he reached into his shirt pocket and pulled out a folded parchment and pushed it across the table. It would've been easier just to push the paper back without opening it, because he knew if he did that something was going to change in his life. Something out of his control.

But he picked up the folded parchment anyway and opened it to discover it was actually three separate pages. He looked at the likeness of the man on the first page and laid it flat on the table. And then he did the same with the second man. Before he looked at the likeness of the third man, the hairs on the back of his nape stood at attention and his gut knotted. He barely noticed Jesse laying a shiny silver star, identical to his own, on top of one of the likenesses.

The third man's face he knew. Almost as well as he knew his own. They shared the same clear blue eyes, dark hair, and crooked smile. And for nine months, they'd shared the same womb. But they'd never shared the same sense of duty or belief in right from wrong.

His brother had always had a look about him that made him seem a little too slick—a little too confident—and Cole had always been wary about trusting him, even though they were flesh and blood.

"He's your spitting image. The government remembers you fondly from the war. You've not only got the skills to fight with guns and your hands, but you've got the skills to fight with your mouth. Without you, the treaties signed with the Sioux might not have happened."

"They offered me an army to command," Cole said, the taste of coffee bitter on his tongue. "And when that didn't work they offered me a position high up, sitting behind a desk and *talking* about how we were going to change things instead of *doing* to change things. I told them no thank you, took the deed to the land they'd offered me, and never looked back."

Jesse rubbed a hand over his beard and then refilled his coffee from the pot the server had left. "Politics can be a pain in the ass. We've all got to deal with it one way or another. There's no such thing as just serving and protecting without strings attached."

Will rolled Jesse's meal out on a cart and placed it in front of him. It was hamburger steak covered in thick gravy and served with mashed potatoes and peas. Normally, Cole's stomach would've been growling, but the thought of food made him sick.

"Enjoy your din…" Will started to say. And then he noticed the silver star on the table. "Holy wow, Sheriff MacKenzie. Is that what I think it is?"

"Marshal Calhoun was just letting me look at it. Don't get too excited."

But it didn't do any good. Will wheeled the cart back to the kitchen as fast as his legs would carry him.

"Congress and the president, of course, are aware of your brother and his efforts during the war, just as they're aware of yours. Though your brother's efforts were quite a bit different than yours," Jesse went on. "It wasn't too difficult to decipher that it was Riley MacKenzie at the helm of The Silver Creek Bandits once his image started making the rounds. But you need to take caution. Bounty hunters and other lawmen might not know you're twins and will be looking for someone fitting your description."

The corner of Cole's lip tilted up in a smile. "We used to trade places when we were kids. Lord, we'd take a beating for it if we were found out. But Riley always liked to test the limits. And I'd found it was a whole lot easier to agree with

Riley than to go against him." Cole had gotten plenty of beatings from his father because Riley hadn't gotten his way.

"He'll come to you eventually," Jesse said. "He's jealous. You're the one who's always recognized. You're the hero. You're the fastest draw. He'll want to challenge that. To see if he can get away with what he's been doing right under your nose."

"And if he shows up in Surrender, I'll meet him on my turf, my way. I don't need to be a marshal to do that."

"It widens your authority," Jesse insisted. "You're one of the best trackers in the country. You learned from the Sioux. You could find him and bring him in. You could find all of them."

Cole shook his head, the realization of his answer sinking in for the first time. There'd always been a conflict inside him when faced with becoming a US Marshal. But knowing what his brother was capable of, and knowing that he had an obligation to protect his wife and community, answered the question for him with a clear conscience.

He pushed the star back across the table. "My place is here, with my wife and this town. My duty is to them first. The job you're asking me to do is meant for a younger man without any ties. I'm not going to pick up and leave my wife for months at a time to track outlaws. There's plenty of good I can do here, with the badge I already have."

"A wife is just a wife," Jesse said. "But this is your chance to go down in history."

Cole laughed. There was nothing *just* about Elizabeth. "I never asked to go down in history. I'm just doing the best I can to make the world we live in the best it can be. I want a family, and I don't want to let them inherit a world of wars and violence."

"War is in the nature of man," Jesse said. "It's been that way since Cain and Abel. And here we are, a whole bunch of years later with the story of two brothers."

Cole had been watching the street, subconsciously seeking out his wife. He was starting to get worried that she'd gotten stuck somewhere. She should've been there by now.

And then, almost as if he'd conjured her, she came through the window of visibility, the snow swirling around her. She'd left her head uncovered, and loose strands of dark hair had come out of the long braid that rested over her shoulder. Her long coat swirled around her legs, and her pistols were slung low on her hips. Unlike any other woman he'd ever met, she chose to wear men's trousers in her day-to-day work at the ranch. He'd never actually seen her in a dress. But he definitely appreciated what she did to a pair of men's pants.

Jesse saw her too, and his fork stopped halfway to his mouth.

"Good Lord," Jesse rasped.

"She's something, huh?"

Jesse blew out a breath and put his fork down. "Oh, good. You see her too. I was afraid maybe I'd died and she was an angel of death."

"There are worse ways to go," Cole said, smiling.

"That's for damned sure." Jesse picked up his fork again, but he'd forgotten what he was doing so he set it down again. "I've got to tell you, MacKenzie, I've seen a lot of things in my life, but I've never seen anything like her."

She was the most beautiful woman he'd ever seen. And she was all his.

"Don't enjoy the view too much," Cole said. "That's my wife." And then he took a closer look. She was mad as a hornet. No wonder she wasn't covered up too much. There was no way the cold was penetrating that kind of anger.

"Damn, son," Jesse said. "I can see why you don't want to leave her to hunt down outlaws."

Chapter Three

Lizzie was so mad she could barely see straight. And then she realized she actually couldn't see because the storm was so bad.

She knew there was no point in letting the likes of Adelaide Murchison get under her skin. But she let it happen every time. And boy, were the things she'd said festering.

Maybe she didn't know what Cole had been up to with his secret meetings. Maybe he was planning to leave because their marriage had grown so distant. Maybe things in Surrender weren't exciting enough for him. Maybe *she* wasn't exciting enough for him. And so what if she didn't have a baby in her belly? It had only been a year. It had taken her mother several years to conceive, and Elizabeth had been their only child.

The cold barely penetrated as she made her way toward the main street and her husband. She almost went to the sheriff's office, but she had a sense that he wasn't there. The lights from the hotel were all she could see through the snow, so she headed straight for them. And then she got close enough to see him through the window, sitting with a man she'd never seen before. But she recognized the type. All lawmen had that look about them.

Adelaide had been right. How did a woman she detested know more about her husband than she did?

Her imagination went into overdrive. What was the real reason Cole wanted to spend two days away with her? Was that how he planned to break the news that he was becoming a US Marshal? Or maybe he planned to give her two last days before he snuck off to hunt down criminals. The territory in Montana, South Dakota, and Wyoming was becoming more and more dangerous. And Cole would be excellent at the job.

She kicked at the step that led up to the sidewalk in front of the hotel. Tears pricked at her eyes and her skin felt like it was on fire. She rarely lost her temper. She'd gotten really good at keeping her anger at bay over the years. Anger about her mother's death. Anger when the ranch hands resented how much time her father spent showing her the ropes of how to run the ranch. Anger that her father had been taken from her much too soon. And if she was honest, anger that Cole had been promised the ranch in name if he'd marry her.

She'd never felt more alone in her life.

"Good evening, Mrs. MacKenzie," Will Clark said from behind the counter. "Your husband..."

But Elizabeth just kept walking into the restaurant, ignoring Will completely, and headed directly to the table her husband was occupying. Cole was watching her with that look he got on his face when he didn't want her to know what he was thinking.

Good grief, he was handsome. It was so easy to get distracted by him. He'd been the only man to ever fill her fantasies. What had started as a childhood crush had ended as a woman's desire for something more.

Cole and the mystery man sat at a square table for four, but she only had eyes for her husband. He was lounging back, relaxed but always ready, a predatory gleam in his crystalline blue eyes. And he was only looking at her. He was tall, his hair dark, and he hadn't shaved before leaving the house that morning, so there was a stubbled beard. His left arm was draped over the chair next to him, but his right arm was always free in case he needed to reach for his weapon.

Maybe she should send Miss Adelaide a thank you card for bringing her back to life. If Cole was leaving, she had nothing left to lose. The only other time she felt this free and alive was when they were making love. That was the *real* her. And Cole was about to get a glimpse of the real her outside of their marriage bed.

She shivered, but held her ground. She'd spent the last year tiptoeing around him, unsure of his reactions and not wanting to confront him about why he'd really married her. She was done tiptoeing.

He smiled at her and she saw the challenge there. She smiled back and wanted to laugh when his own smile disappeared. Cole MacKenzie didn't know her. Not really. He knew the brittle woman who'd thrown herself into hard labor for the past year to keep from falling apart over her father's death. He knew the woman who never lost her temper.

Both men stood as she approached the table, and she caught a glimpse of the shiny marshal's badge that was on the table and felt her stomach clench.

"Elizabeth," Cole said. "I want to introduce you to Marshal Jesse Calhoun. He's come to visit Surrender for a couple of days."

Elizabeth gave Calhoun a cursory glance and said, "It's a

terrible time to visit. We're having a blizzard. I hope you don't have anywhere to be for a few days. Maybe even a couple of weeks."

Jesse smiled at her and nodded his head. "I'm sure I'll find Surrender quite hospitable. No matter how long I need to stay to accomplish my task."

Elizabeth nodded, understanding the unspoken words. Calhoun wasn't planning to go anywhere unless her husband was with him.

"I was just at the bank," she said, changing the subject. "Miss Adelaide said a marshal had come to town to swear you in as one of their own."

"Ahh," Cole said, his lips quirking in a half smile. "Miss Adelaide is always up to date on current events. And she always has such pure intentions."

"I feel like I'm missing something," Jesse said.

"Is she right?" Elizabeth asked, ignoring Jesse. Her gaze didn't waver from her husband's. "Are you going to become a US Marshal? Are you leaving?"

"Your husband is an incredibly valuable asset to the government," Jesse answered before Cole could. "And The Silver Creek Bandits are wreaking havoc across the country. Their death toll is at fifty-eight."

"And at last count," she said, her voice raising slightly, "four of those deaths have been other US Marshals. No one has been able to stop them. I'd prefer my husband wasn't thrown to the wolves because the government has run out of people to sacrifice."

Jesse smiled indulgently and her blood boiled. "That's not something for you to worry about, Mrs. MacKenzie. There are extenuating circumstances with the deaths of those marshals.

But your husband is a man who can take care of himself."

"You don't have to explain my husband to me," she said. "I know that he's a man of honor. And I know that he can take care of himself. That doesn't make him immortal."

"I think this is something my wife and I need to discuss in private, Calhoun."

"Take your time, MacKenzie. It doesn't look like I'm going anywhere any time soon. But the president doesn't want me to return without that star pinned to your vest."

"You're not married, are you, Calhoun?" Cole asked.

"Never had the time," he said.

"Then I'm going to take into account your inexperience and save you from getting stabbed in the face with your butter knife. You should stop talking now and enjoy the rest of your dinner. And my wife and I are going to go upstairs and talk in private."

Jesse looked back and forth between them and shrugged, and then he took his place back at the table to finish his meal.

Elizabeth watched as Cole folded up the likenesses that had been on the table and shoved them into his pocket. He left the badge where it lay and nodded to Calhoun as he took her arm and picked up the bag they'd packed that morning.

She resisted the urge to shrug off Cole's touch, and she let him guide her out of the restaurant. She continued to stay silent when he got the key to their room from Will, who was standing wide-eyed and slack-jawed behind the desk.

It wasn't until they'd reached the second-floor landing that she found her voice again. "How did you know I wanted to stab him?" she asked.

"I recognized the look. I've never told you much about my family. There's not much that's worth telling. But I've learned to recognize a woman who's reached her breaking point. And in my experience, a woman who's reached her breaking point when there's a knife around will use it."

She stopped on the bottom step that led to the third floor and stared at him in surprise. He'd been right when he'd said he hadn't shared much about his family. She knew he had a brother, but she didn't even know his parents' names.

"Your mother stabbed your father?" she asked incredulously.

"Twelve times," he said flatly. "She wanted to make sure he was really dead. I don't even know how she lifted the knife. He'd broken her arm and several ribs beating on her. I walked in on her. She was sitting on the floor, propped against the wall like a ragdoll, covered in his blood. He'd beaten her so bad something punctured her on the inside. The doctor said she bled to death."

Elizabeth put her hand on his arm as he tried to keep moving up the stairs. "I'm so sorry. I had no idea."

"Why would you?" he asked. "That was another life. Another time."

"You're making it hard to be mad at you right now," she said.

"I'm sorry I'm missing out on it," he said with a grin. "I saw that look in your eyes when you walked in and all I could think about was getting you upstairs and in bed. Your father always said you had a hell of a temper when riled. I've waited for a year to see it. Maybe I could do something else to get you riled back up."

"I might have left the knife downstairs, but I'm still wearing my guns. Proceed at your own risk."

"My, my, my, Mrs. MacKenzie," he said, moving in close

behind her as they reached the top of the stairs. "What have you been holding out on me?"

Her breath caught as he maneuvered her to the door of their suite and pressed against her. She felt his breath on her neck and his hardness against her backside as he turned the key in the lock and opened the door.

She hadn't forgotten why they'd come upstairs to begin with, and it definitely wasn't for this, no matter how badly she needed to feel his touch. His lips glanced the side of her neck and she groaned, even as chill bumps pebbled her skin.

The room was nice and warm, and it looked as if Will had started a fire in the fireplace. She'd never stayed at the hotel before. There'd never been a reason to. But the rooms they'd been assigned were much nicer than anything she'd ever seen. The carpet was plush under her feet and the woods of the furniture dark.

There was a small sitting room with a couch and two chairs in front of the fire, and the windows looked out over Main Street, though it was impossible to see anything but the falling snowflakes. She turned and walked toward the bedroom.

It wasn't a large room—or maybe the bed was so large that it made the room seem small. It had four posts of the same carved, dark wood as the rest of the furniture. The bed was covered in a white quilt and looked soft as a cloud. And above the bed was a painting of a woman, scantily clad. Elizabeth raised her brows at the scandalous nature of the artwork and wondered why she'd never heard talk of it around town. But then, it made sense that the people who lived in Surrender wouldn't be staying in the hotel, just like her.

There was a washroom to the side, and she peeked inside,

surprised to see the deep porcelain tub and gold faucets.

"I've never seen anything like this in my life," she finally said. "Can we afford this?"

"It depends on your definition of afford."

Her head snapped around to look at him in surprise. She'd thrown everything she had into the ranch the past year—the breeding and selling of cattle, the upkeep on the fences and barn. From the moment she and Cole woke in the morning to when they lay in bed together at night, she worked herself to the bone. When she was working, it was easier to forget that she felt like she was carrying the weight of the world on her shoulders.

She knew the ranch was in the black. The bookkeeper kept her up to date on the finances. But she also didn't have a clue as to how much in the black they were. What was left to spare. And she had no earthly idea what Cole brought in as sheriff, though it seemed people paid him more in favors, like food and supplies he might need.

"I'm kidding," he said. "Gerald Clark owes me a favor or two. The season hasn't started because of all the snow. The train hasn't been running as usual, so there haven't been new guests. The room was available, so he said to take it for a couple of days."

"Oh." She felt very awkward all of a sudden. The emotions she'd felt earlier were still there—the anger and hurt—but they'd faded once she and Cole were alone. "That was nice of him."

"These two days," Cole began, "they're really important to me, Elizabeth. We have a lot to talk about. I think you'd agree that the last year of our marriage hasn't really been a marriage at all."

Elizabeth's heart sank. This was it. This was when he'd end it. When he'd tell her he was leaving. She braced herself for it, and hadn't realized she'd sat on the edge of the bed and closed her eyes.

"I guess that's my fault," she said. "I'm not really sure how to be married. My mom died when I was so young..."

"And you think I do?" he asked, sounding surprised. "I just told you about the kind of marriage my parents had. Believe me, that didn't exactly imprint visions of happily ever after on my mind."

She scrubbed her hands over her face and got to her feet, and then crossed her arms over her chest. Anger was bubbling beneath the surface and she paced back and forth.

"This is my father's fault," she said. "You got trapped into marriage because of your sense of duty. You knew what would happen to me and everything he and my grandfather built if I didn't have a husband. So you agreed to his ridiculous terms and put all your own dreams on hold. It's made me realize I don't even know you. I didn't know of your plans to become a marshal. I only know about your time in the war because people like Miss Adelaide like to spread the worst of things. Of course, I don't believe most of what she said, but there's probably a shred of truth in there somewhere, otherwise the president wouldn't be trying to recruit you. She knew about the marshal who'd come for you today. Why didn't you tell me? Were you going to pin on your badge and send me a letter from somewhere in Wyoming?"

"Elizabeth," Cole said, coming to her. He put his hands on her upper arms to keep her from pacing. Her body was quivering with everything she'd kept inside all this time. "First of all, let's set something straight."

Before she knew what was happening, his mouth was on hers and every thought in her head rushed out of her ears. She remembered the first time he'd kissed her, at their wedding, and she understood there was something powerful in the connection they shared that she never would've understood if her father hadn't negotiated her marriage to Cole.

His lips were soft, his mouth hot against hers, and she sank against him, as if her body had a will of its own. It was easy to close her eyes and just *feel*. To hold on and let their bodies meld together. This was when she felt closest to him, when she felt she really understood him. When their bodies were joined and they were perfectly in sync.

When he pulled away they were both breathing heavily and she could barely stand. "Let's get two things straight before we move forward. I never wanted to be a marshal. I put down roots in Surrender because this is where I wanted to be. This is the life I want. I've turned down every marshal that's come to pin that star on me. This one won't be any different."

"There have been others?" she asked, surprised.

"Three others. And my answer has always been the same. This is my home. You are my wife. My family. I've never had a family before. At least not a real one."

"You said there were two things," she said. "What's the second?"

"The second is that your father didn't have to persuade me to marry you. I don't remember when exactly I took notice of you. One day you were a child and then one day you weren't. It was like being slammed in the face with a piece of wood. You're not like any woman I've ever known. Looking at you is like staring at a single, beautiful rose in a garden of weeds. I knew if I noticed you, that others had noticed you too."

"I have no idea what you're talking about right now," she said, confused.

He released her and ran a hand through his hair. "I'm not good at explaining myself. I've never had to do it before, but I can see that's where I made the mistake with us. We haven't exactly done a good job at communicating."

He turned and walked away and she could sense his frustration. But she'd found her tension and worry had eased as soon as he'd told her he had no plans to become a US Marshal. She followed him into the sitting area, but she'd observed him enough to know he'd talk when he was ready.

Elizabeth unbuckled her holster and set it on the table in front of the windows and then she used the boot pull in the corner to remove her boots. The wind was howling, and the snow was blowing sideways. The street was impossible to see.

He was silent for so long his voice surprised her when he finally spoke again. "When your father came to me and asked if I would marry you, I thought he was giving me the best gift anyone could've ever given. And not because the ranch would be deeded to me upon his death. He knew he was sick, and his only thought was to make sure you were taken care of. And he picked me to see out what he couldn't."

She didn't realize she was crying. She couldn't remember the last time she had. Everything had happened so fast. She'd only thought her father was fighting off a bad cold. But he'd gotten increasingly worse over just a couple of weeks. He'd lost weight and could barely take a breath, and there was nothing any doctor could do. He just wasted away right in front of her eyes.

She hadn't had time to cry. Someone had to take over his

duties when he'd been too sick to do them himself. She'd been the one to do that. In between taking care of her father, work had consumed her. And then he'd died, and work had still consumed her. The care of the animals and the day-to-day operation of the ranch couldn't stop.

Her foreman had taken over so she could see to all the funeral arrangements. And then there were papers to be signed and his estate to see to. So the day after her father had been put in the ground, she and Cole had married. And then life went on. There hadn't been time to cry.

Cole moved close to her and placed his hand upon her cheek, wiping away tears with his thumb.

"He was one of the best men I've ever known," Cole continued. "I wish he would've been my father. You don't realize how lucky you were."

"I do," she said softly. "I miss him every day." She leaned into his hand slightly and then moved away to stand in front of the fire and warm her chilled hands.

"When he came to me, it was almost like he was warning me against agreeing to what he was asking. He said you were independent, hot-headed, and smart-mouthed. He told me you were loyal to a fault and had a great capacity for love. He told me you worked harder than any man he'd ever known, and that the ranch was your joy. And that if I were to marry you, that I should never dim your joy. I've done everything he asked, but I failed at the one thing that was most important to him. You've had no joy over the last year of our marriage."

"That's not true," she said, turning to face him. "Don't you understand that you have been the *only* joy I've felt over the last year? My whole life has been turned upside down. My father was all I had after my mother died. And he did the best he could. He showed me what it meant to love and care for the ranch. To know the importance of what he and my grandfather had worked so hard for. To instill pride in my legacy, so that legacy can be passed on to my own children— our children—for generations to come."

She rubbed at her arms, but she found she couldn't quite look him in the eye when she mentioned children. Adelaide's words about her not conceiving yet had pierced deep.

Her mouth was dry, but she continued. "And then, just like that, he was gone. And I was left with the ranch, the only thing besides my father that I'd loved for all the years when it had been just me and him. But working the ranch every day only made me realize the absence of my father. There's been no joy there. But there was you," she said. "The only time I've felt anything the past year is when I'm with you. I...love you. I've loved you since I was twelve years old. My dad somehow knew that. I don't want you to leave. And I know that's selfish. Why would you want to stay?"

Cole moved in fast and close and grasped her arms. "Are you kidding me? Why *wouldn't* I want to stay? You're my wife. All I know is you walked by the sheriff's office one day, and I stopped everything I was doing, mesmerized."

He smiled and the corners of his eyes crinkled. "I went outside to get a better look and got to witness you giving the blacksmith a hell of a dressing-down."

"He shortchanged my order," she said defensively.

"And I'm sure he never did it again," Cole said. "Needless to say, I started paying a lot more attention to you after that day. Believe me, your father was nobody's fool. I'm sure he noticed my interest. He'd come by the sheriff's office and just sit in the chair in front of my desk, passing a long, thoughtful silence before he'd utter a word. Then we'd just talk. He was my friend."

Elizabeth took in a big gulp of air, and she realized she'd been holding her breath. But then it turned into a sob.

"Please don't go," she said, dropping her forehead onto his chest. "Miss Adelaide said you would go, and that there was no reason to stay because I didn't even have a baby in my belly."

"Miss Adelaide has made a habit of sticking her nose where it doesn't belong. Maybe she needs to be given a warning about disorderly conduct."

She sniffled out a laugh and then relaxed in his arms. It felt good to be held. It felt right. But it didn't go past her notice that he hadn't uttered the words she'd needed to hear, though she felt they'd made tremendous strides during their conversation. Perhaps, over time, he'd be able to tell her the words.

"I have an excellent idea," he said, twining his arms around her. His mouth found the sensitive spot beneath her ear and her heart started pounding.

"Umm…"

"It's amazing how you can never find your words when I do this," he said, blowing against her neck.

"Ahh…"

He laughed and bit the lobe of her ear. And then he found her mouth, taking it deep, their tongues melding and passions rising. He walked her into the bedroom, never taking his lips from hers, disrobing her a piece at a time. When he laid her back on the white cloud of the bed, worshipping her body with his mouth and touch, she felt the love he hadn't spoken.

Chapter Four

"What were those papers on the table?" she asked some time later. "The ones you and the marshal were talking about?"

The lantern next to the bed was turned down low, emitting a soft, yellow glow across the room. They'd managed to make it under the covers at some point, and Elizabeth lay across his naked chest, her fingers stroking his shoulder.

She felt his sigh, and he moved to sit up. She rolled to her back and watched as he flipped back the covers and got out of bed. It was pointless to pretend she wasn't watching him. His body was fascinating to her. And her inexperience in bed had made her timid when it came to exploring his body. But he'd encouraged her, telling her to touch him how she wanted, and telling her what pleased him.

Now she was more curious than ever. And anxious to do it again. His body was beautiful. He was tall and broad, the muscles in his shoulders a fascination to her. She felt the heat rising in her cheeks as her gaze lowered. He was completely comfortable in his nakedness.

"If you keep looking at me like that we won't end up having this conversation until much later."

He searched on the floor for his shirt and found the papers folded in his front pocket.

"Marshal Calhoun came all this way because the Silver Creek Bandits have escalated. They think my expertise in tracking, and my ability with a gun, might help them locate the gang and put an end to them once and for all."

He handed her the folded papers and she opened them slowly, wondering at the unusual heaviness of the parchment.

"Their last hit was in Denver, and a witness managed to give a likeness rendering before The Silver Creek Bandits killed him and his entire family."

Elizabeth looked through the images in front of her, and then she froze as she came to the last image. Her blood chilled.

"I don't understand. Why are you in here?"

"I told you I had a brother," Cole said. "What I didn't tell you is that he's my identical twin."

"Oh, my God." It didn't take her long to see the possibilities. "They're going to think it's you."

"No, no," he said, coming over to her and sitting down on the bed. "The government knows about Riley. They have a file on him. I told you that we didn't have a real family growing up. Let's just say that Riley took after my father more than I did. After our parents' deaths, we went our own ways. Until the war."

A look came over Cole's face that made her realize he'd gone back to those days, remembering whatever horrors he'd lived through.

"The Black Hills War was a nightmare. Right from the start. The government was so determined to take that land from the Sioux. But those of us who were fighting, who saw the atrocities that happened, knew it was wrong. It's a hell of a thing when right and wrong interfere with duty.

"I guess I'm lucky," he said, blowing out a breath. "Things could've gone much worse for me than they did. I managed to make friends with the Sioux. To keep them protected. So they knew where the ambushes would occur. In return, they taught me how to hunt and track like they did. And when the time came, I approached our government with the idea for a treaty between the US and the Sioux. Luckily, we were able to end the war with a peaceful resolution."

She reached out and took his hand. "You could have been killed. From either side. That was incredibly brave."

"Bravery is a lot more appealing when you're young and have nothing to live for. My brother must have felt the same, but he worked from the other side of things. He sold secrets to whoever paid him the most. Because of him, entire Sioux families were wiped out. Women, children... It didn't matter to him as long as the gold was real.

"They never caught him. He was always a step ahead. Which is why I'm not surprised he's had such success as the leader of The Silver Creek Bandits. They think I'll be able to find him because I know how he thinks and where he'll go."

"And where do you think he'll go?" she asked.

"I think he'll come looking for me. It's just another reason that I need to stay here."

There was a loud pounding at the door and she jerked in surprise. It wasn't late in the evening yet, about the time they usually ate dinner, but things were quiet because of the storm. She'd felt safe and cocooned inside their temporary lodgings.

"What the hell?" Cole said, grabbing the blanket from the end of the bed and wrapping it around his waist.

He headed toward the door, and she wasn't about to be left out. She grabbed the blanket off the rocking chair and her pistol from her gun belt, and then she stood out of the way as Cole went to the door.

"Who's there?" he asked.

"It's Calhoun. We've got a situation. And it's not a good one. We need guns. Any you can muster up."

"I'll be down in five and you can fill me in," Cole said, dropping his blanket and moving toward his clothes on the floor.

"I'm going with you," Elizabeth said. "And before you argue, he said you need all the guns you can get. You know I'm better than anyone else in the area. It's going to be hard to find people to go out during this storm."

She dropped her blanket and started putting on her clothes, not waiting for Cole to answer her. Whatever was happening was bad. She couldn't imagine the marshal would come to them for any other reason.

"I wasn't going to argue with you," he said. "I was going to say hurry."

Her smile was grim, but she was glad he believed in her enough to let her go. She'd lived a life unlike most. She was used to the harsh winters, but she was also used to the harshness of life. She'd dealt with having to put down animals to ease their suffering, but she'd also seen the atrocities of what men could do to one another. She'd dealt with thieves and rustlers. Her father had known the importance of teaching her how to protect what was hers.

Once they were dressed they went downstairs, ignoring Will once more and heading outside, where Marshal Calhoun was waiting for them. The wind and snow blasted them in the face, and icy knives pierced her lungs with every breath she took.

"This is madness, Calhoun," Cole said loudly. "Nothing can be bad enough to venture out in this weather."

"That's where you're wrong," he said. "The others are meeting us at your office."

Elizabeth could only see a few feet in front of them, so it wasn't until they were almost there that she saw the light on at the jail and the smattering of dark figures inside.

"After dinner," Calhoun continued, "I walked across to the saloon for a drink. After an hour or so a man burst in. Jenkins, I think, was his name. Small, doughy fellow."

"He's an attorney. He and his wife settled here from back east."

"He was white as the snow and shaking so bad it was hard to understand him, but we got some whiskey down him and he was able to get it out. Poor bastard. Said his wife never came home from running errands."

"Oh, no," Elizabeth said. "But I saw her at the bank as I was leaving. She was near the back of the line. Do you think she got lost in the blizzard? They're not from here. It would be easy to get turned around."

"Unfortunately, no," Calhoun said. "Jenkins had talked to her just before she left for the bank, so he knew where to trace her steps. When he got to the bank, the door was locked, but all the lights were still on. The shades were pulled on the front windows, so he walked around to the back. That's when he saw the carnage."

"Spit it out, Calhoun," Cole said as they stepped under the protective covering over the sidewalk. "What happened?"

"The Silver Creek Bandits are in Surrender," he said.

"Every last person in that bank was murdered."

Cole reached down and grabbed her hand, and Elizabeth felt the breath squeeze out of her lungs. *Everyone. Murdered.*

"That's impossible," she said. "I was there. Just as they were about to close." And then she remembered the man who had walked in as she was leaving. She'd not looked at him because she'd been so angry. But it *had* to be him.

"Then consider yourself lucky to be alive," Calhoun said. "Did you see anyone who didn't belong? Anyone on the street as you were leaving?"

"There was a man who was coming in as I was leaving, but he was by himself. I was so mad from the argument I'd just had with Miss Adelaide that I couldn't see straight. I didn't notice anyone on the street, but it was already snowing pretty hard by then. I just wanted to get away from there."

She closed her eyes as Calhoun's words sunk in. They were gone. All of them. Leroy Henry and Samuel Peabody. Mrs. Jenkins and Isabelle Pert, who been standing just behind her. Frank Daniels, the barber, and Josiah Newton, the postmaster. And Adelaide Murchison, a woman whose last time on earth was spent hearing hurtful words. From her.

"The tracks are still fresh," Calhoun said, interrupting her thoughts. "But they're fading quickly. This is the best shot we have to run them down."

"Then let's not waste any time," Cole said. "Have the men saddle up."

* * * *

The anticipation of battle had always made Cole more aware of his surroundings. He became focused and able to shut out the noise around him. But this was the first time he'd ever been to battle with Elizabeth at his side. It was the first time he wondered if he'd be able to focus because he'd be worried about her.

This was between him and Riley. He knew it and Calhoun knew it. Hell, Calhoun probably knew The Silver Creek Bandits were in the area. Marshals weren't stupid and they had a hell of an instinct. Cole had known this day would come. He hadn't known about Riley and what he'd been doing, but he knew his brother would find him some day. They were two sides of the same coin.

"Get what you need from inside," he told Elizabeth. "You know where the rifles are. And I've got a couple of extra furs you can layer up with. Every second we waste those tracks are disappearing."

Elizabeth nodded and went inside, and Cole headed with the other men to the side of the building where the horses had been brought around. They were all men who knew the right end of a gun, including the gunsmith, who'd provided many of the weapons they were using on short notice. The blacksmith had also rigged up an iron rod at the back of each saddle, and a lantern hung from the hook at the top. They'd need every bit of help they could get. They were all familiar with the territory, but it would still be easy to get lost in the snow and darkness.

Elizabeth came out with a rifle in each hand and a fur poncho thrown over her coat. A fur-lined cap was pulled down over her ears. She tossed him an extra fur poncho and cap, and then strapped her rifle onto the back of her saddle before tossing him the other rifle so he could do the same.

His horse, Goliath, was the grandsire of the horse he'd ridden in battle. He was pure onyx, with three white marks across his forehead, and his coat was thick and used to Montana winters. Goliath snorted out a breath and stamped his hoof, sensing the excitement in the other horses, as Cole mounted him.

He moved to the head of the group, and there was an eerie quiet as white swirled around them and the horses' steps were silenced by the snow. It was a short ride to the bank, and Calhoun came up beside him as he motioned for the others to stop. The lights were still on, as Jenkins had said, and Cole could only imagine what waited for them inside. But they couldn't tend to the dead yet. Not when their killers were still on the loose.

"The tracks start around here," Calhoun said, motioning his horse forward. "I can see at least three sets of footprints and horses, but could be more if they were following in each other's paths."

"There's five," Cole said. He stared at the tracks and blocked out everything around him until he could recreate what had taken place there, just as the Sioux had taught him. He had to become one with the prey to find the prey, and that's exactly what his brother was—*prey*. Nothing more, nothing less.

They were fortunate in that the snow that had already been on the ground previously had been several inches deep, and a couple of more inches had fallen before his brother had left the bank. The footprints they'd left were deep, and if he had to hazard a guess, Riley had timed the robbery with the storm, hoping that their tracks would be completely covered before the bodies were found.

And they almost had been. In another hour, they'd have been left with nothing. But the storm hadn't quite made it to its full potential yet.

"Stay armed and vigilant," Cole called out to the others. "They'll have found a place for shelter. They can't have gotten too far. Not with it getting dark and with the snow. We don't want to lose any more tonight. If something feels off then tell me. If something seems out of place, speak up. We know this area better than these bastards, and they've taken the lives of our own. We bring every one of them in. Dead or alive."

There was a chorus of angry grunts, and they set off, going as quickly as they could without compromising the tracks. Riley was smart. It wasn't past him to circle back around and let them follow the tracks until they walked into an ambush.

Half an hour later, he got a sickening feeling in his gut. Riley hadn't circled around to try and outsmart them. He'd had a plan. He knew exactly where he was going.

"Cole," Elizabeth said, riding up close beside him. "What's going on? We're getting too close…"

"I know," he interrupted. He could see the fear in her eyes. The fear that everything they'd worked for, her legacy, and their children's legacy would be gone. He was afraid she might be right.

Chapter Five

He smelled the smoke before they reached the ranch, and he had to pull on Elizabeth's reins to keep her from charging ahead to her death.

Riley had been in the area long enough to know where they lived, to know the workings of the ranch.

"Damn," Cole said. "You hired that new hand about a month back."

Her eyes widened as they locked with his. "Wyatt? You think he's a member of The Silver Creek Bandits? He's just a baby."

"Old enough," Cole said.

"I can't believe we had him living on our property all this time."

"It makes sense. It's why there were only five sets of tracks back at the bank instead of six, like all the witness reports had given. The sixth man was already here, making sure everything was ready for them to take over when the rest of the gang got here. You and I made plans to get away for a couple of days more than two weeks back. They knew this was the perfect time."

They were still a good mile from the ranch, and though they couldn't see where the smoke was coming from, the stench was heavily mixed with the snow. His blood chilled at the thought of more lives being lost.

"What's on fire?" Calhoun said, coming up beside him and Elizabeth.

"At a guess, either the barracks the hands sleep in or the barn."

"I take it you know where we are?" Calhoun asked.

Cole's fingers tightened on the reins. "Yeah, welcome to Cold Creek Ranch. My wife and I would invite you to stay for the night, but it seems we have some uninvited guests."

"Ahh," Calhoun said. "He found you."

"So it seems. Our foreman hired a man a few weeks back, and our best assumption is he's one of the gang, and planted himself here to feed information to Riley."

"It follows their pattern. They haven't gone this long without being caught because they were stupid."

"There's always a first for everything," Cole said. "Now we have to figure out how the hell to get them off our property and behind bars."

"We can use the storm to our advantage. They've got shelter, but they won't be able to see us approaching. We need to split up and surround the house. It's twelve against six."

"You think he'll make it that easy?" Cole asked. "If that's the case we can bar the doors and burn the house down."

"Are you crazy?" Elizabeth interrupted. "That's our house. Everything we own is inside."

"That's my point. They won't trap themselves inside of a place they can't get out. Not unless they really think we won't find them until the storm passes. In that case, we might just get lucky."

The men had circled around him to listen to what was being said. The tracks were no longer visible, and several inches of snow had fallen since they'd set out on their journey. There was a soft glow of light in the center of the circle.

"Pair up in twos," Cole said. "But only use one lantern. Most of you know the layout of our ranch. If you don't, get with someone who does. My guess is the barracks are on fire, so stay clear. You don't want to be detected due to the light from the fire. These men are smart. They've evaded the law for more than three years. And don't let your guard down because there's only six of them. They'll be waiting for you. We don't need any more bloodshed unless it's theirs.

"Chances are they'll be split up, a couple in the house and some in the barn. There's also an outbuilding that holds tools a hundred paces or so west of the barn, but it's an unlikely hiding place. The storm is on our side. Use it to your advantage. It'll be hard for them to see you until you're almost on top of them, and there's not a lot of places to hide for cover.

"The marshal will take a team to surround the house, and I'll take another team to the barn. No gunfire unless absolutely necessary. We want to keep our cover as long as possible. Good luck and Godspeed."

They lined up side by side and rode the remaining mile in silence. The wind and snow was blowing directly at them, and they were all hunkered with their faces down. Cole didn't see the rider coming toward them until they were almost on top of each other, and he had his gun out and cocked just as the man waved his arms.

Cole's fingers were stiff and aching from the cold, but he

didn't lower his pistol.

"It's me," Lester McCoy yelled.

"Lester," Elizabeth said, moving her horse forward to embrace him.

Lester had been the foreman for the ranch since before Elizabeth was born, and since her father's death, he'd taken on a fatherly role. She would've been devastated if anything had happened to him.

"What happened?" Cole asked, coming up beside them. He noticed the soot and blood that covered Lester's face.

"That bastard Wyatt betrayed us. We were busy getting the animals settled and racing against the storm. We had some cattle get loose we had to track down. By the time we got back to the barracks for supper, the storm was already in full swing. Wyatt waited until we'd all sat down with our food and then he barred all the doors.

"When we first smelled the smoke, we thought Cookie was burning something in the kitchen. But then the smoke got stronger and it started filling the room. Everyone hustled for the door but we couldn't get it open. And then Seamus gave it a good kick with his boot and Wyatt was waiting right there for him with his shotgun. Seamus took the bullet right in the chest."

Lester shook his head, and there was anger in his eyes. "We had no choice but to go back inside and try to get out another way. Every time one of us would break a window, Wyatt would shoot off a shell right at us. We finally ran back through the kitchen where the fire was worst and took our chances with the flames. The whole thing was coming down at that point. I took a knock on the head," he said, pointing to where the blood was coming from.

"Wyatt wasn't alone by the time we got out. There were five others with him, and I swear I thought one of them was you, Sheriff. He was the spittin' image, but his clothes were fancier. City clothes. All of them were dressed for the city. Had some polish to them."

"My brother always had a taste for the finer things," Cole said.

"Brother?" Lester asked. His expression grew thoughtful and his mouth pressed in a straight line. Snow and ice clung to his mustache and brows. "Well," he finally said. "That's a hell of a thing. Wouldn't want to be in your shoes right about now."

"Blood doesn't make you family." Goliath shifted impatiently beneath him. "What happened after you escaped the barracks?"

"They started shooting, but they was shooting blind. I always keep my pistol on me, and it's the same with a couple of the others, but we were outgunned and we knew it. They had the advantage, but we know the land, so we set off for the hunting cabin and put as much distance between us as possible."

"Why'd you come back?" Elizabeth asked him. "You're taking a terrible risk."

"The only chance we had was if one of us went into town to find you. There's no telling how long the storm will last, but once the snow stops I figured they might come looking for us. Or worse, the two of you would come home and walk right into an ambush.

"I snuck down from the cabin to see what was what, and went straight to the barn to make sure they hadn't done anything to the animals or the structure. I crept around the barn to see if I could get a glimpse of them, but they weren't anywhere to be seen. All our stalls are full because of the storm, so they just left their horses loose downstairs to feed and bed down. I was able to get the barn door open a crack and one of their horses was right there. Managed to get him out without being noticed. But I could hear people talking up in the loft. I got out of there fast as I could. And this is how far I made it. Feel like I've been out here for days."

"You're still armed?" Cole asked.

"Of course."

"Fall in line. We could use all the men we can get. You just met The Silver Creek Bandits."

There was a large tree that Elizabeth's grandfather had planted in the crook where the road split and the long driveway toward the ranch began. The tree had withstood many storms, and it would withstand this one.

They started up the drive, and about halfway along Cole signaled Calhoun to take his men in the opposite direction. Their time was limited. Their bodies and the horses could only last so long in the elements. If their plan failed, they'd all be holed up in the hunting cabin for the night. And taking the bandits out would be harder and probably cost more lives.

When he and those who had followed him reached the split-rail fence, they veered to the right to circle back around the barn. They'd put out all but a couple of their lanterns, and visibility was almost impossible. He used the fence as a guide until they reached the paddock and the barn came into view.

There were no lights, other than the lanterns they used.

"We've got to flush them out," Cole said. "They have the advantage being up high. I need you all to circle around and wait. They'll try to escape somehow, and they're likely to come out shooting. Be ready."

"Wait," Elizabeth said, grabbing his arm. "What are you doing?"

"I'm going in there," he said. "If I can sneak in and take them by surprise, there's a better chance of keeping our boys alive."

"You're not going in there by yourself. You'd be outnumbered."

"This is what I'm good at," he promised her. "They'll never know I'm coming."

"Then I'm coming too. I won't let you go in there by yourself. You keep saying how smart they are. Don't you think they'll have planned for something like this? Especially Riley. Doesn't he know what you're good at as well as you do?"

He knew she had a point, but his gut instinct wanted to protect her. Not put her in harm's way.

"You'll stay with me," he agreed. She was shivering beneath the warm layers of her coat and wrap. They couldn't fight the cold much longer.

"We can't use the outside ladder," she said. "They'll have someone watching the hayloft entry."

"No, we'll have to slip in through the barn door, just like Lester did. The wind is howling so fiercely the barn will already be creaking and groaning."

He moved to dismount Goliath and she put her hand on his arm. "Wait," she said, biting her lip to keep it from shivering. "What about the old barn?"

He looked at her, confusion on his face. "What about it?"

"I just have a bad feeling about this, trying to outsneak a sneak. He knows you. He's counting on you coming after him, blizzard or not. This is exactly the kind of trap he wants to catch you in."

"I don't see another way," he said. He had trouble keeping the frustration out of his voice. Time was wasting.

"What if chaos is the best way to draw him out?" she asked. "What he wants in the end is to test his skills against yours. You said he's as good with a gun as you are. He wants a showdown. He wants to prove he's the best there is."

"I don't understand what you're saying. Our guns are the only weapons we have to defeat him."

"That's not true," she insisted. "They're trapped. He put them on high ground because he thought he knew what you'd do. He's waiting for you to come to him, when he needs to come to us. I say we open the barn doors. Make as much noise as we can and get the animals to scatter. And then I say we set the barn on fire and smoke them out. We'll block the entrances and wait for them."

His immediate instinct was to ask her if she'd lost her mind, but he closed his mouth before the words could come out. He didn't know if they had a chance in hell of beating Riley, but he knew the odds were against him if he had to face off against his brother. His fingers were half frozen and his reflexes were sluggish from the cold and fatigue.

"Have I told you how much I love you?" he asked, mesmerized by her. This woman was his wife, and she amazed him on so many levels. He'd never understood what it meant to love a person that much. Yes, he could live without her. He'd been without that kind of love until he met her. But he was so much better *with* her in his life. She was strong where he was weak, and he complemented her the same way.

She was staring at him as if he'd grown a second head.

"What's wrong? Why are you looking at me like that?"

"Now's when you pick to tell me you love me?"

Her voice was hoarse and sounded as if she'd swallowed shards of glass, and her face was pale, though he wasn't sure if it was from shock or the cold. Tears pricked her eyes, and he was really starting to get concerned. What had he done wrong?

"Do you know how long I've waited for you to say those words?"

Red streaks appeared on each cheekbone and her eyes narrowed. Lord, she was mad. But he couldn't understand why.

"I've told you I love you before," he said.

"Don't lie to me! If you do anything, always tell me the truth."

"I'm not lying," he said, sitting up a little straighter in his saddle. "I tell you in bed every night before I go to sleep."

If fire could shoot out of a person's eyes, he was pretty sure he'd be nothing more than bone dust.

"You…" she started and then tried again. "You…you…"

Before things got out of hand he reached across and plucked her out of her saddle and into his lap. "I'm only going to say this once because we're about to freeze to death and we've got a gang of robbers who've taken over our home. But I love you. I whisper it in your ear every night before I fall asleep. And whenever I do you snuggle closer and squeeze my hand. *You're* the one who's never said it to me."

She stopped squirming in his arms and stared at him in wide-eyed shock. "You must be out of your mind. I've never heard you say it."

"Maybe your ears haven't, but your body sure has. You know what it's like to tell someone you love them and have them squeeze your hand in response? It's not a good feeling.

I've been waiting for you to say it back for months."

"I love you too," she said hotly.

He couldn't help it. He laughed. What were they doing? They must both be crazy.

"I loved you before your father ever stepped foot in my office. I would've asked you to marry me if he hadn't beaten me to it. I've fought in war, and I've seen terrible things. Enough to make you lose hope in people. But you're my heart."

She was so still in his arms he wasn't entirely sure she was breathing. But then her gloved hand gently touched the side of his face. "You're my heart too. And I hate to interrupt this moment. But we need to go burn down our barn."

"This is going to make a hell of a story someday."

"No one would believe it," she said.

Chapter Six

It took little time to inform the others of the change in plans, and there was an anticipation—an eagerness—that hadn't been there before. There was a hope that they might all come out of this alive.

Two of the men had gone to intercept Calhoun and the others and let them know what was happening. More than likely, once the chaos started anyone holed up in the house would come out to see what was going on. That's when they'd be taken down. And all without shooting holes in her house. Hopefully.

Elizabeth's heart was lighter than it had been since before her father's death. Cole loved her. They could iron out all the other details later.

There were two entrances to the barn, one on each end to get the animals in and out as efficiently as possible, depending on where they were being taken. But order was the last thing they wanted.

They'd divided the men into two groups for each end of the barn. The horses were restless, the anticipation thick in the air as the swirling snow blew around them. She knew what her job was. It was to eliminate as many threats as possible so the men could accomplish their task.

She dismounted from her horse and carried her rifle easily in her right hand. She sank to her knees in the snow, but was long past feeling the cold. Anger was fueling her warmth. This was her life and her property that were being threatened, and it was her husband that Riley MacKenzie was targeting.

Her pistols were within easy reach in her holsters, and she watched as Cole dismounted from Goliath. Both of their horses were smart enough to get out of the way. They could feel the unrest in the air.

Cole looked at her and she nodded, and then he lifted the latch for the barn doors and swung them wide. They swooped in with shouts and gunfire, shooting their pistols in the air to get the animals moving. The doors from the other side were opened and a bitter wind blew through the main corridor, sending bits of hay flying along with the snow.

The animals panicked, braying and bucking against their stalls. The horses Riley and his gang had left loose took off like a shot, and other horses soon followed as their gates were opened. They'd left the lanterns lit, hanging from hooks inside the barn, and the yellowish hue cast shadows over the confusion.

It would've been easy to be distracted by the chaos, but she kept her eyes on the ladder up to the loft. It was wide with wooden slats, and it led into a large square hole in the upper floor—large enough to bring hay up or down when needed. It was there, right at the corner, that the light from the lanterns reflected off the barrel of a gun.

Cole was across from her, hidden beneath the rafters, and he wouldn't see what she could see from his angle. Her father had enjoyed quoting Benjamin Franklin's saying about an ounce of prevention being worth a pound of cure, and this seemed as good a time as any to take matters into her own hands.

She cocked the shotgun and took a brief moment to sight before pulling the trigger. Wood exploded at the entrance to the loft and a body tumbled straight down to the base of the ladder. She heard a shout and realized the animals had all been evacuated, then there was more gunfire as one of the men shot at the lantern in the far corner. It exploded into pieces of glass and sparks, and the embers fell into the hay on the ground, causing a small smolder before the embers caught flame.

It wasn't long before the flames grew, and she felt a small pang at the loss of the barn she'd helped to build with her own two hands, right alongside her father.

"Everyone out," Cole yelled.

Smoke filled the air and she backed out of the barn with the others, catching her husband's eye as he exited the opposite end. They closed the barn doors and then moved back out of the way as the flames licked the walls and started burning in earnest. Black smoke curls snuck through the cracks in the doors and wood.

She heard gunshots from over toward the house, but she ignored them, instead running around the barn to where Cole was. Cole was the target. Wherever he was, Riley would search him out.

It hadn't taken long for the fire to consume the barn. It was a readymade tinderbox, and the flames lit the sky, even in the midst of the blizzard. As she turned the corner to find Cole, she felt something heavy land behind her, but before she could turn, an arm was around her neck and she was dragged backward.

She fought against her captor, but her heels slid as she tried to dig them in. His arm tightened around her neck, and she struggled to breathe. And then she realized she'd dropped the shotgun somewhere in the snow.

"Elizabeth!" she heard Cole yell.

But her gaze was transfixed on the hayloft door. Black smoke billowed out, but she saw the outline of the man standing in the doorway. And then he was gone as he jumped straight down into the snowdrift below.

He was dead before he hit the ground.

Cole didn't waste any time taking the extra man out. The danger was Riley, and it would do no good to have a showdown with his brother only to have someone else shoot him in the back. There was no honor among these thieves.

"Let her go, Riley," Cole called out. "This is between you and me. You want to be the best? Then it's time to show me what you've got."

"Or I could just kill her and you too."

His voice was so much like Cole's, it sent a chill down her spine.

"There's a dozen guns on you right now," Cole said. "If you kill Elizabeth you'll die very quickly. But it won't be the kind of death you want. You'll never know if you could beat me. And you and I both know that's all this is about. It's always been a game to you, Riley."

"Of course it's always been a game," he mocked. "How many times growing up was I just a little too slow? Or not quite as perfect as you were. I wouldn't expect you to notice because it wasn't your face that was feeling his fist every time I failed."

"I felt his fist plenty," Cole said. "You could've been different. But you're just like him. *Worse* than him. The slaughter of the innocent was your choice. You chose to make it into a game. To put me at the blame instead of him."

"It sure felt right to blame you when I was the one doubled over with a broken rib or two. But it doesn't matter now. We went our separate ways. And I worked until I was as good as you were. And I worked some more until I was better. And now here we are.

"We always were more alike than you wanted to admit. You've got a dark side, Cole," he sneered. She could see the clouds from his breath as he spoke next to her ear. "I saw that firsthand during the war. I wonder, did you ever feel me tracking you like the Sioux taught you to track?"

"I knew you were following me," Cole said. "You could've tried to kill me then."

"Wrong time, wrong place. The Sioux were rather protective of you. Besides, I had things to do before I could come back for you, brother."

"What things?" Cole asked.

"I'm a very wealthy man."

"There's a lot of blood on that money."

"There's a price for everything," Riley said. "But like you said, this is between you and me. Call your men off. Because once I kill you I'm going to borrow your wife as insurance until I get to where I'm going. I don't want her dying too soon because one of them got trigger happy."

"It's not my men you'll have to worry about if you kill me," Cole said.

Elizabeth could see the half smile on his lips and wondered why he'd pick now to taunt his brother. But then she saw the subtle movement of his hand, and a frisson of fear skittered down her spine.

He couldn't be serious. She shook her head to tell him no, but Riley squeezed his arm tighter around her neck. Cole made the movement with his hand again, and she realized he was dead serious. The smile left his face and he stood squared off against his brother. And then she realized what he was trying to tell her. She felt the movement to Riley's right side, where he pushed his coat back so he could get to his pistol.

Riley had no intention of letting her go. He planned to draw on Cole while he was holding her captive, in hopes that Cole wouldn't draw on him in fear of hitting her. Riley had no honor, and if she didn't do as Cole asked and give him a fighting chance, then they'd both end up dead. All she could do was trust Cole. With her life.

"I'm warning you, Riley," Cole said. "Let her go. You'll never know if you can beat me unless we face off. Nothing between us but our guns."

"Yeah," Riley said, and she could feel his body tense as he shifted his weight slightly. The lying, cheating bastard. She'd be damned if she let him get away with this. She didn't care if she had to throw her body in front of his gun.

She kept her eyes on Cole's hands, waiting for the signal. Just the slightest twitch of his fingers and she went limp. Two guns fired and she was jerked backward. She waited for the searing pain of a bullet wound to bring life to her numb body, but she felt nothing but the cold as she hit the ground.

"Cole," she tried to scream, but her voice was hoarse. She'd heard two shots and she'd felt Riley draw. He'd shot at Cole.

Elizabeth rolled to her hands and knees and tried to

scramble to her feet, but her legs had turned to jelly. She couldn't see Cole. She couldn't catch her breath. And she couldn't imagine a life without her husband in it.

Tears clouded her vision and snow swirled around her. She was completely blind as she felt her way through the snow. She touched a leg and worked her way up the prone body, and her hands shook as she wiped her eyes and leaned closer. A sob tore from her throat as she saw her husband's face. But then she realized the man she was staring at—the man whose skin was as ashen as the sooty snow around them—wasn't her husband after all.

She'd never seen Riley MacKenzie in person, other than the likeness Cole had shown her. Their similarities were remarkable. But there were slight differences. And this man was *not* her husband. But her husband could be as dead as Riley.

A strength she didn't know she possessed rose up inside of her, and she came to her feet with a roar. And then she ran face-first into a hard chest.

"My God, Elizabeth," Cole said, wrapping his arms around her. "You scared the hell out of me."

"I can't believe you shot at me," she said. And then she broke down sobbing in his arms.

"I shot around you, darling. That's entirely different."

"That's all of them, boss," one of the men called out. "The Silver Creek Bandits are dead."

"Everyone head to the house and get warm. Nothing we can do about the barn. We can get the animals settled in a bit."

"Lester's already taking care of it," Calhoun said. "Better get your woman inside before she gets frostbite from all those tears. I got to hand it to you, son. That takes absolute brass balls to shoot at a man who's holding your wife. One wrong move..."

Elizabeth pulled back from Cole's arms, but he scooped her up and started walking toward the house. The barn was still in full flame, but it was far enough away from their other buildings as to not be a danger. Cole was right. There was nothing they could do about the barn but watch it burn.

She looked up at her husband and her breath caught in her chest. He was so big and strong. And so hers. And most importantly, he loved her.

They had tough days ahead. They had friends to bury and rebuilding to do. But as long as they had each other, they could get through anything.

"Cole," she said, touching a hand to his face. He stopped and looked down at her. His eyes were tired and his face drawn. Killing his brother had more of an impact than he was letting on, and there would be grief and healing to tend to in the coming days and weeks.

"Why are you looking at me like that?" he asked.

"Because I love you. Because you make me proud. Because this is a moment that will be passed down in story to our children and grandchildren, and I want to remember exactly how I felt as you held me in your arms."

"There is no greater love," he said, his voice husky with emotion.

Epilogue

One Year Later...

"I can't do this," Elizabeth said.

Cole watched her battle for every breath as the life within her fought to come into the world. She was soaked with sweat and exhaustion showed in the darkness beneath her eyes. The pain had lasted for hours, and he could see the worry on the doctor's face as night had turned to day, and then back to night again.

He took her hand and grimaced as she squeezed hard enough for the bones to crack as another contraction wracked her body. The fire burned hot in the hearth and the doctor tried to keep thick blankets over her, but she kept kicking them off. He'd never felt so helpless in his life. He'd already bucked the doctor's orders by staying in the room with his wife. But after the first several hours, he questioned his sanity. The need to go out and get drunk with Lester and the rest of the hands was starting to sound like a good idea.

"Elizabeth, really," Doctor Jones said. "You must keep

covered. You don't want the baby to catch a chill when he's born."

"Get out," she said, pushing the covers off again. She tried to sit up, but her weight was too bulky and she was too uncoordinated, so Cole put an arm behind her back and helped her sit up some.

"Get out!" she said again when Doctor Jones just stood there, staring at her as if she'd lost her mind. Then she turned to Cole. "Please."

"Give us a few minutes," Cole told him.

"That's unwise, Sheriff. Things can sometimes happen rather quickly. This is typical of a woman giving birth. I've plenty of experience with this. They don't know what they want when the pain overtakes them. They don't have the same constitution that we men have."

At that moment, he questioned the sanity of Surrender's new doctor. He'd never seen a warrior, not in battle or anywhere else, who was fighting like his wife was.

"It'll be fine," Cole said as diplomatically as he could. "I'll call you back when we need you. Bessy has some fresh coffee on the stove. Help yourself."

Cole made the command clear this time. If Elizabeth wanted the doctor out for a little while, then she could have it. She'd earned it. And there was a part of him that was afraid he might never get time alone with his wife again. Even he knew that this wasn't normal. That she couldn't keep going like she was.

The door closed behind Doctor Jones, but his gaze stayed on his wife.

"I hate these covers and I hate that fire. It's too hot. I can't even breathe."

"The doctor said…"

"I don't care!" she yelled. "Surely you can see by now that he's a moron."

Cole winced because it was for sure the doctor now knew Elizabeth thought him a moron. She started kicking the covers off, and Cole decided that he'd do anything she asked of him, no matter how unreasonable. If by chance these were her last hours on earth, then he'd do whatever it took to make her happy.

He helped her remove the covers and then her flannel nightgown so she lay naked on the bed. Her stomach was impossibly round and taut, and her breasts swollen to twice what they'd once been. She was beautiful. And he felt part of his soul breaking at the thought of losing her.

"Can you open the window?" she asked. "Just a little."

He had to admit that the room was stifling. He was stripped down to his undershirt and still soaked to the skin. He couldn't imagine how she must be feeling doing all the work. A cold swirl of air entered the room as soon as he opened the window, and he saw her visibly relax for the first time in hours.

He moved back to the side of the bed and sat on the stool there, waiting for whatever was next. Words of encouragement stuck in his throat. He didn't know what else to say.

"I think I'm going to die," she finally said, a calmness and finality to her voice that terrified him beyond belief.

"No," he said. "I won't let you."

She laughed and sweat beaded on her forehead, despite the goose bumps forming on her body from the cold air.

"Sometimes even your stubbornness can be defeated."

"Not in my experience," he said. "Now stop talking about

it. The baby can hear you."

"You sound as looney as Doctor Jones."

He watched in fascination as another contraction gripped her and her stomach moved, tightening to impossible levels. He placed a hand on her belly and let her squeeze his hand. And when it was over she dropped back against the pillow and panted for breath.

He leaned over and placed a kiss on her belly, and then while he was there he closed his eyes and said a prayer. This was his life. His world. And he begged God not to take it away from him.

He kissed her belly again and felt the movement of life beneath his lips. He hardly noticed that his cheeks were wet with tears.

"What are we going to name him?" he asked.

"Riley," she said, without hesitation.

He jerked back in surprise. "What? That's not funny, Elizabeth."

"I'm not joking. This baby is the start of a new generation of MacKenzies. He's our future. The start of our legacy. And this Riley will be the kind of man who knows how important family is. He'll have honor and integrity. And he'll pass on to his children and grandchildren that nothing is more important than family."

Cole's tears flowed freely now, and he brushed the wet hair back from her forehead with his fingers. "He's the start," Cole agreed. "A new legacy will be born tonight. And it'll continue for generations to come. I love you more than life itself, Elizabeth MacKenzie."

He leaned forward to kiss her, and her arms twined around his neck. He'd only meant it to be a short kiss, but she surprised him, taking him deep, her tongue sliding sensually against his.

"We can't do this," he said, pulling away. "It can't be good for you."

"I don't care," she said. "If I'm going to die, I want to remember the feel of your mouth against mine. I want your lips on me. Please. Just for a little while. I don't feel the pain when you're kissing me."

He couldn't deny her. Not when tears clung to her lashes and defeat was in her eyes. He leaned forward and took her lips again, ignoring the need of his own body. The closer she'd gotten to her time, the less frequently they'd made love. His need for her was fierce, but his need to please her was greater.

His lips trailed down her neck and she arched back, giving him full access. But he didn't stop there. He kissed his way down to her breasts, full and round and heavy, her nipples darker than they'd once been, and his lips circled around a taut nipple, his tongue laving it before he suckled gently.

Her gasp of pleasure was music to his ears and her fingers grasped in his hair, holding him close.

"Oh, God," she gasped. And then he heard a rush of water and her grip tightened painfully on his hair.

"The baby's coming," she said, straining to sit up. "He's coming right now. I have to push."

Elizabeth still had a grasp on his hair, so he extricated her fingers carefully so he could move into a position to see if the baby was really coming. There wasn't time to call for the doctor. Almost before he was able to position himself between Elizabeth's legs, he was holding his son in his arms.

The lusty cries of a baby brought the doctor running into the room. He barely kept it together at the sight of a fully naked Elizabeth, and then he immediately headed to the window to close it.

"Well then," he said. "It seems you handled things just fine. You'll want to nurse the baby as soon as you can to get your milk flowing."

Cole almost laughed at the pink that crept up Elizabeth's cheeks. If the good doctor could've brought himself to look at his wife, he would've seen firsthand that her milk was already flowing just fine.

Bessy, their housekeeper, had come in behind Doctor Jones and took the baby from him, cleaning him up and wrapping him in a blanket. The doctor worked on Elizabeth, got her cleaned up, and Cole helped her into a new nightgown. And before he knew it, they were alone with their son.

"Riley John MacKenzie," Cole said, deciding his son should share his middle name with Elizabeth's father. And when he looked into deep blue eyes, the same as his, he knew he would lay down his life for the child in his arms.

He placed him in Elizabeth's arms and watch the baby root at her breast. And he felt a peace wash over him. This was his family. A real family. This was a new beginning.

"This is the start of our legacy," he said, his voice hoarse with pride. "From this day forward the MacKenzies mean family."

"Our family," Elizabeth said. "Now kiss me. I can't keep my eyes open any longer."

"I'd never argue with the mother of my child."

She laughed and said, "I'll remember that the next time you want to argue about something."

"Maybe you'll forget I said that just like I'll forget your promise to never let me touch you again."

"Well… It seemed a good idea at the time," she said. They were both laughing as their lips touched.

* * * *

Also from 1001 Dark Nights and Liliana Hart, discover Sweet Surrender, Captured in Surrender, Trouble Maker, Spies and Stilettos, and The Promise of Surrender.

Sign up for the 1001 Dark Nights Newsletter
and be entered to win a Tiffany Key necklace.

There's a contest every month!

Go to www.1001DarkNights.com to subcribe.

As a bonus, all subscribers will receive a free
1001 Dark Nights story
The First Night
by Lexi Blake & M.J. Rose

Discover 1001 Dark Nights Collection Four

Go to www.1001DarkNights.com for more information

ROCK CHICK REAWAKENING by Kristen Ashley
A Rock Chick Novella

ADORING INK by Carrie Ann Ryan
A Montgomery Ink Novella

SWEET RIVALRY by K. Bromberg

SHADE'S LADY by Joanna Wylde
A Reapers MC Novella

RAZR by Larissa Ione
A Demonica Underworld Novella

ARRANGED by Lexi Blake
A Masters and Mercenaries Novella

TANGLED by Rebecca Zanetti
A Dark Protectors Novella

HOLD ME by J. Kenner
A Stark Ever After Novella

SOMEHOW, SOME WAY by Jennifer Probst
A Billionaire Builders Novella

TOO CLOSE TO CALL by Tessa Bailey
A Romancing the Clarksons Novella

HUNTED by Elisabeth Naughton
An Eternal Guardians Novella

EYES ON YOU by Laura Kaye
A Blasphemy Novella

BLADE by Alexandra Ivy/Laura Wright
A Bayou Heat Novella

DRAGON BURN by Donna Grant
A Dark Kings Novella

TRIPPED OUT by Lorelei James
A Blacktop Cowboys® Novella

STUD FINDER by Lauren Blakely

MIDNIGHT UNLEASHED by Lara Adrian
A Midnight Breed Novella

HALLOW BE THE HAUNT by Heather Graham
A Krewe of Hunters Novella

DIRTY FILTHY FIX by Laurelin Paige
A Fixed Novella

THE BED MATE by Kendall Ryan
A Room Mate Novella

PRINCE ROMAN by CD Reiss

NO RESERVATIONS by Kristen Proby
A Fusion Novella

DAWN OF SURRENDER by Liliana Hart
A MacKenzie Family Novella

Discover 1001 Dark Nights Collection One

Go to www.1001DarkNights.com for more information

FOREVER WICKED by Shayla Black
CRIMSON TWILIGHT by Heather Graham
CAPTURED IN SURRENDER by Liliana Hart
SILENT BITE: A SCANGUARDS WEDDING by Tina Folsom
DUNGEON GAMES by Lexi Blake
AZAGOTH by Larissa Ione
NEED YOU NOW by Lisa Renee Jones
SHOW ME, BABY by Cherise Sinclair
ROPED IN by Lorelei James
TEMPTED BY MIDNIGHT by Lara Adrian
THE FLAME by Christopher Rice
CARESS OF DARKNESS by Julie Kenner

Also from 1001 Dark Nights

TAME ME by J. Kenner

Discover 1001 Dark Nights Collection Two

Go to www.1001DarkNights.com for more information

WICKED WOLF by Carrie Ann Ryan
WHEN IRISH EYES ARE HAUNTING by Heather Graham
EASY WITH YOU by Kristen Proby
MASTER OF FREEDOM by Cherise Sinclair
CARESS OF PLEASURE by Julie Kenner
ADORED by Lexi Blake
HADES by Larissa Ione
RAVAGED by Elisabeth Naughton
DREAM OF YOU by Jennifer L. Armentrout
STRIPPED DOWN by Lorelei James
RAGE/KILLIAN by Alexandra Ivy/Laura Wright
DRAGON KING by Donna Grant
PURE WICKED by Shayla Black
HARD AS STEEL by Laura Kaye
STROKE OF MIDNIGHT by Lara Adrian
ALL HALLOWS EVE by Heather Graham
KISS THE FLAME by Christopher Rice
DARING HER LOVE by Melissa Foster
TEASED by Rebecca Zanetti
THE PROMISE OF SURRENDER by Liliana Hart

Also from 1001 Dark Nights

THE SURRENDER GATE By Christopher Rice
SERVICING THE TARGET By Cherise Sinclair

Discover 1001 Dark Nights Collection Three

Go to www.1001DarkNights.com for more information

HIDDEN INK by Carrie Ann Ryan
BLOOD ON THE BAYOU by Heather Graham
SEARCHING FOR MINE by Jennifer Probst
DANCE OF DESIRE by Christopher Rice
ROUGH RHYTHM by Tessa Bailey
DEVOTED by Lexi Blake
Z by Larissa Ione
FALLING UNDER YOU by Laurelin Paige
EASY FOR KEEPS by Kristen Proby
UNCHAINED by Elisabeth Naughton
HARD TO SERVE by Laura Kaye
DRAGON FEVER by Donna Grant
KAYDEN/SIMON by Alexandra Ivy/Laura Wright
STRUNG UP by Lorelei James
MIDNIGHT UNTAMED by Lara Adrian
TRICKED by Rebecca Zanetti
DIRTY WICKED by Shayla Black
THE ONLY ONE by Lauren Blakely
SWEET SURRENDER by Liliana Hart

About Liliana Hart

Liliana Hart is a *New York Times*, *USA Today*, and Publisher's Weekly Bestselling Author of more than 50 titles. After starting her first novel her freshman year of college, she immediately became addicted to writing and knew she'd found what she was meant to do with her life. She has no idea why she majored in music.

Since self-publishing in June of 2011, Liliana has sold more than 5 million ebooks and been translated into eight languages. She's appeared at #1 on lists all over the world and all three of her series have appeared on the *New York Times* list. Liliana is a sought after speaker and she's given keynote speeches and self-publishing workshops to standing-room-only crowds from California to New York to London.

Liliana can almost always be found at her computer writing, or spending time with her husband and five children.

Connect with me online:
twitter.com/Liliana_Hart
https://www.facebook.com/groups/lilianassweetharts/
My Website: www.lilianahart.com

Discover More Liliana Hart

Sweet Surrender
A MacKenzie Family Novella
By Liliana Hart

It's been twelve years since Liza Carmichael stepped foot in Surrender, but after her great aunt's death she has no choice but to return and settle her estate. Which includes the corner bakery that's been a staple in Surrender for more than fifty years.

After twenty-five years on the job, Lieutenant Grant Boone finds himself at loose ends now that he's retired. He's gotten a number of job offers—one from MacKenzie Security—but he's burned out and jaded, and the last thing he wants to do is carry the burden of another badge and weapon. He almost turns down the invitation from his good friend Cooper MacKenzie to stay as their guest for a few weeks while he's deciding what to do with the rest of his life. But he packs his bag and heads to Surrender anyway.

The only thing Boone knows is that his future plans don't include Liza Carmichael. She's bossy, temperamental, and the confections she bakes are sweet enough to tempt a saint. Thank God he's never pretended to be one. But after he gets one taste of Liza and things start heating up in the kitchen, he realizes how delicious new beginnings can be.

* * * *

Captured in Surrender
A MacKenzie Family Novella
By Liliana Hart

Bounty Hunter Naya Blade never thought she'd step foot in Surrender, Montana again. Especially since there was a warrant out for her arrest. But when her skip ends up in the normally peaceful town, she has no choice but to go after him to claim her reward. Even at the cost of running into the cop that makes her blood run hot and her sense of self-preservation run cold.

Deputy Lane Greyson wants to see Naya in handcuffs, but he'd much prefer them attached to his bed instead of in a cold jail cell. She drove him crazy once before and then drove right out of town, leaving havoc in her wake. He's determined to help her hunt down the bad guy so he can claim his own bounty—her.

* * * *

The Promise of Surrender
A MacKenzie Family Novella
By Liliana Hart

Mia Russo spent ten years working undercover, entrenched in the dregs of society before handing in her shield. Opening her own pawn shop is a piece of cake in comparison. All she needs is the bad attitude she developed on the streets and the shotgun under her counter to keep law and order. Until the day Zeke McBride walks into her shop.

Zeke knows Mia has every right not to trust him. He was the one who chose the next op instead of her. And all he can hope is that somewhere under the snarl and cynicism is a woman who can forgive. Because whether she trusts him or not, they're going to have to work together to bring down the gang that's decided Mia is their next target.

* * * *

Trouble Maker
A MacKenzie Family Novel
by Liliana Hart

Marnie Whitlock has never known what it's like to be normal. Her ability to see the future and people's innermost thoughts makes her an outcast—feared—loathed. Even by her own parents. And her father is determined to beat the curse out of her. Her only chance for survival is to escape Surrender.

Beckett Hamilton has loved Marnie since they were kids, but one horrible night destroyed any future he'd hoped for. Now Marnie was back in Surrender, and picking up where they left off is the only thing on his mind. He finds out quickly that some hearts take longer to heal, and not everyone that's broken can be fixed. But loving Marnie isn't an option—it's his destiny.

* * * *

Spies & Stilettos
A MacKenzie Family Novel
by Liliana Hart

New York Times bestselling author Liliana Hart returns to her bestselling MacKenzie family with her trademark of "Passionate Romantic Suspense & Spine-Tingling Mystery" in SPIES & STILETTOS...

Elena Nayal has worked for MacKenzie Security for years. Quiet and unassuming, she stays in the shadows of the world's most elite clandestine agency. But she's trained relentlessly after hours, and her only thought is to be strong enough to track down and kill every last one of the men who brutally attacked her.

Lieutenant Brady Scott is no stranger to special ops. He commands the greatest SEAL team in the history of America. But fighting for the woman he loves turns out to be the most difficult mission he's ever been on. He must decide whether to let her walk into a suicide mission on her own, or ignore every rule he's sworn to follow.

On behalf of 1001 Dark Nights,

Liz Berry and M.J. Rose would like to thank ~

Steve Berry
Doug Scofield
Kim Guidroz
Jillian Stein
InkSlinger PR
Dan Slater
Asha Hossain
Chris Graham
Fedora Chen
Kasi Alexander
Jessica Johns
Dylan Stockton
Richard Blake
BookTrib After Dark
and Simon Lipskar